This Book Belongs To

Kayleigh,
You're very special like
"Twinkle-Dust."
Fondly,
Alin W. Bowman
MARCH 2001

Given By

Date

Published by:

BIG FOOT PUBLISHING

P.O. Box 511
Liverpool, NY 13088

Copyright ©1993 by Alice W. Bowman
All rights reserved.

Fourth Printing 2000, Revised

ISBN: 0-9645870-6-8

Library of Congress Catalog Card Number 95-78256

Printed in the United States of America
November 2000

Other "Twinkle-Dust" Adventures by Alice W. Bowman:

 On his arrival in the Eastern Galaxies, where the adventure begins, TWINKLE-DUST is greeted with a pleasant surprise. His friends are there waiting to help him. They work together to triumph over the dangers they meet unexpectedly along the way. Learn how TWINKLE-DUST, with the help of his friends, carry out God's assignment; to lead the Wisemen from the East to God's Son. $6.95

 During the Sonic Bowl Game #40, TWINKLE-DUST is called to the Chambers of God for his next assignment. Before long, with the help of a star ballerina named Stariel, TWINKLE-DUST and his friends master one routine after another. After the dazzling performance, TWINKLE-DUST is once again summoned by God. He is told that his dazzling light is needed to blind Saul on the road to Damascus. $6.95

 God sends TWINKLE-DUST and his friends to planet Earth on a working vacation. They arrive in Lake Placid during the Winter Games. At nighttime the stars have fun racing down the ski trails. During the day they rest while the Olympic athletes perform. Learn how TWINKLE-DUST and his friends turn a working vacation into A COOL ADVENTURE for everyone. $6.95

 At the end of the Mars Madness Basketball Championship game, Twink's beeper went off. A message from God told Twink that, in the morning, he would fax to him and his friends their next assignment. When the fax arrives, everyone is anxious to get started. Twink, his friends and others are to help in the rescue of passengers from the sinking ship, the TITANIC. Enjoy this new adventure. As you read, you will learn how teamwork played an important part in the rescue, and how even those who appeared to be losers became the true winners. $8.95

Prices and availability subject to change without notice.

**To order these exciting adventures contact BIG FOOT PUBLISHING
at the above address or telephone 1-800-284-7514 (access code 01).
www.Twinkle-Dust.com**

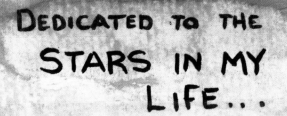

DEDICATED TO THE
STARS IN MY
LIFE...

... MY GRANDCHILDREN

ASHLEY

PHILIP

ALISON

ILLUSTRATIONS BY AND DEDICATED TO TIFFANY AND ALYSSA
HOLLY L. PELELLA

The Galaxy Hospital waiting room, located on Milky Way, was buzzing with excitement. Everyone was happy to hear that Stella had become a mother. They heard the new papa was so excited he was jumping up and down with joy.

Suddenly, Papa pushed open the door. Papa spoke so fast not one of them understood a word he said.

"Calm down," Starbert, a friend, said. "Please tell us again, but this time slower."

Papa began, "Wait till you see our baby star. He was born with gold dust dancing around him. There was so much light that the doctor and nurses were startled. They knew a 'Special Star' had been born; yet each wondered the reason for this unusual birth. Stella and I are so happy that whatever it is, we plan to teach him in the ways of God. In time, God's plan will be made known for our Twinkle-Dust. Oh, by the way, that is the name Stella and I have chosen for him, *"Twinkle-Dust."* Isn't that a perfect name?" said Papa.

The hospital intercom clicked on.
"Mr. Star, you, your family and friends can now go
to the nursery to visit your wife and newborn son."

They all hurried off to see Twinkle-Dust.

They found Mama looking through the nursery window smiling at her precious bundle of joy. Now all of them stood and looked through the window. Not one of them had trouble spotting Twinkle-Dust. There in a bassinet, everyone could see gold dust dancing around a little sleeping star. They were delighted. Each one wondered about this "Special Star."

Their thoughts were interrupted by Papa. "Stella," Papa said. "I talked with the doctor. I know this is unusual, but I am to take you and Twinkle-Dust home tomorrow. Twinkle-Dust is growing. The gold dusting is much, much brighter. Now the nurses are afraid the other baby stars will have trouble sleeping in the nursery."

A troubled look appeared on Mama's face. Was this a warning of things to come?

The next day the family left the hospital. Mama carried Twinkle-Dust and Papa led them to their "Star-Mobile." On the way home, Papa stopped at Star-Aid to buy a pair of small dark glasses.

"Stella," Papa said, "just in case Twinkle-Dust has trouble sleeping, I bought these glasses to hide the glare of the gold dust. They should help." Papa was already thinking ahead. He wanted so much to be a good papa.

The years passed quickly. Soon Twinkle-Dust would be going to school. By now, he was much bigger than all his cousins and friends. The gold dusting had brightened. Oh, how Twinkle-Dust had first hated, hated to play hide-and-seek with his friends. This was a game he dreaded playing. How could he hide? His friends could see him a galaxy away.

The bright light gave away his hiding place every time until Papa helped him. Papa made Twinkle-Dust a black coat that zipped up the front, hiding all the gold dust. It helped until Twinkle-Dust grew bigger and bigger and bigger. Then the other stars made fun of him. They yelled, "Twinkle, Twinkle BIG, BIG STAR, we don't wonder where YOU ARE."

Twinkle-Dust would go home crying. Mama wiped away his tears.

Then she held him in her arms and said, "Twinkle-Dust, you mustn't let the other stars bother you. God has a plan for you. In time you'll know what it is. Just be patient." Mama's words cheered Twinkle-Dust.

Then in school, there were new problems. Twinkle-Dust sat in the back of the room in order not to bother the other stars. If a film was shown, he had to stand out in the hall. It was impossible to see a movie in his bright light. Over the years Twinkle-Dust had to make many changes, but he never gave up. He just prayed for the day when he would know why he was created "SPECIAL."

Then in the sixth grade, the class studied the universe - the galaxies, the planets and the stars.

Twinkle-Dust was so excited when he came home. "Mama! Mama!" Twinkle-Dust shouted. "Guess what we studied in school?"

Mama was surprised. She had never seen Twinkle-Dust like this. He said, "Today we studied the stars. Oh, Mama, it was so interesting. We studied the Little Dipper, the Big Dipper and, and the North Star. Mama, did you know that the North Star guides all the ships on planet Earth? Mama, as the teacher taught, a strange feeling warmed my heart. Do you think someday I might be a star that leads? Do you, Mama, do you?"

Mama answered, "Twinkle-Dust, this could be it. Already your friends look up to you as their leader. And then when you exercise, you become so much brighter. In time, if this is God's plan for you, He will make it known. You must be patient till that time comes."

Twinkle-Dust was so happy that he kept this thought of becoming a leader deep in his heart. No longer was he upset by his size or his brilliance.

At last the day came. Upon graduation with honors from Galaxy University, Twinkle-Dust was called to the chambers of God. This was the long-awaited day. Why were his star knees trembling? Why was his throat so dry? Would he be able to ask God all the questions bothering him?

As Twinkle-Dust went into God's chambers,
an awesome feeling of peace came over him.
Twinkle-Dust no longer had any questions.
He waited upon GOD...

"Twinkle-Dust," God said. "I have created you for a very, very 'Special' assignment. Soon My Son will be born on Earth. Your assignment is to lead the Wisemen from the East. They are coming to worship Him bringing gifts of gold, frankincense and myrrh. As you lead them closer to Bethlehem, Herod the King will be interested in their search. Your light will dim for a short time, but then you will shine brighter. Go, Twinkle-Dust, for your time has come to lead."

And so Twinkle-Dust left the chambers of God. He kept a journal telling of his "awesome adventure." His brightness led the Wisemen to God's Son. Truly, Twinkle-Dust was a "Special Star." He continues to lead, for above manger scenes, honoring the birth of the Christ Child, the star shining ever so brightly is God's Twinkle-Dust.